The Checkup

For Dr Sharma

PUFFIN PIED PIPER BOOKS
Published by the Penguin Group
Penguin Books USA Inc., 375 Hudson Street, New York, New York 10014, U.S.A.
Penguin Books Ltd, 27 Wrights Lane, London W8 5TZ, England
Penguin Books Australia Ltd, Ringwood, Victoria, Australia
Penguin Books Canada Ltd, 10 Alcorn Avenue, Toronto, Ontario, Canada M4V 3B2
Penguin Books (N.Z.) Ltd, 182–190 Wairau Road, Auckland 10, New Zealand
Penguin Books Ltd, Registered Offices: Harmondsworth, Middlesex, England

First published in hardcover in the United States 1983 by
Dial Books for Young Readers
A Division of Penguin Books USA Inc.
Published in Great Britain by Walker Books, Inc.
Copyright © 1983 by Helen Oxenbury
All rights reserved
Library of Congress Catalog Card Number: 83-5346
Printed in Hong Kong
First Puffin Pied Piper Printing 1994
ISBN 0-14-055275-8
1 3 5 7 9 10 8 6 4 2
A Pied Piper Book is a registered trademark of
Dial Books for Young Readers, a division of Penguin Books USA Inc.,
® TM 1,163,686 and ® TM 1,054,312.

The Checkup

by Helen Oxenbury

A Puffin Pied Piper

Mommy took me to the doctor
for a checkup.
"You'll have to wait your turn,"
the nurse said.
The waiting room smelled funny.
I opened the window.

Nobody wanted to talk to me.
"Maybe they're not feeling well,"
Mommy whispered.

"Who's next?" the doctor asked.
"Come on, it's our turn," said Mommy.
"I want to go home," I said.

"Well, young man, shall we listen
to your chest?"
I sat on Mommy's lap.
"See," Mommy said, "it doesn't hurt."

"If you do what the doctor says,
    I'll buy you something on the way home,"
Mommy whispered.

"Let's go home now, Mommy," I said.
The doctor fell off his chair.

"Call the nurse!" said the doctor.
"I'm so sorry," said Mommy.

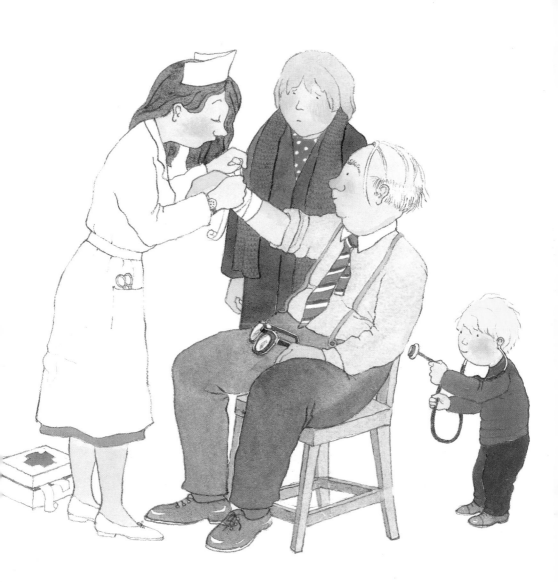

"He seems normal enough,"
  the doctor said. "I won't have to see
  him for another year, I hope."
"I like the doctor," I said.
"I think he's really nice."

About the Author/Artist

Helen Oxenbury is internationally recognized as one of the finest children's book illustrators, with over thirty books to her credit, including *We're Going on a Bear Hunt* and *The Dragon of an Ordinary Family* (Dial) by Margaret Mahy. Her Very First Books®—five board books for toddlers—have been newly designed and reissued by Dial. According to *The Washington Post,* the books "will delight parents and entertain infants." *The Bulletin of the Center for Children's Books* applauded, "Fun, but more than that: These are geared to the toddler's interests and experiences." Ms. Oxenbury lives in London.